Crocodile Smile

10 Songs of the Earth as the Animals See It

Written and sung by Sarah Weeks

Illustrated by Lois Ehlert

A Laura Geringer Book An Imprint of HarperCollins*Publishers*

TUFTED-EARED
MARMOSET

Piece of Jungle

We all need piece of jungle
Tree to climb
And vine to carry us home
Yes, that's what jungle is — home.

We all need piece of jungle
Space to clear
And place for making new home
Yes, that's what jungle is — home.

Home to orchid
Home to moth
Home to tree toad, snake, and sloth
Lemur and muriqui swing by
Under same blue sky.

Same sky
Same trees
Same sweet breeze.

We all need piece of jungle
Fruit to eat
And nest of family at home
Yes, that's what jungle is — home.

We all need piece of jungle
Thatch for roof
And rain to hurry us home
Yes, that's what jungle is — home.

Home to cheetah
Home to bat
Home to human wearing hat
Monkey and machete swing high
Under same blue sky.

Same sky
Same trees
Same sweet breeze.

We all need piece of jungle
Peaceful little piece of jungle
Every piece of jungle —
Someone's home.

Pretty Tree

GIANT PANDA

Allow me to introduce myself
You probably don't know me
See, I don't get out that much
I just sit in my pretty tree
Sit in my pretty tree
Eating the tasty bamboo
Sit in my pretty tree
Eating the sweet bamboo.

My mama's a giant panda
My papa's a panda too
There used to be lots of pandas
But now there are very few
Sitting in pretty trees
Eating the tasty bamboo
Sitting in pretty trees
Eating the sweet bamboo.

Do you hear (chop! chop!)
That funny sound? (chop! chop!)
What could it be?
So nearby (chop! chop!)
It shakes the ground
Under my pretty tree.

We live in the bamboo thicket
With nothing but rain to fear
We play in the swaying branches
We're all very happy here
Sitting in pretty trees
Eating the tasty bamboo
Sitting in pretty trees
Eating the sweet bamboo.

There it is again (chop! chop!)
That funny sound (chop! chop!)
What could it be?
So nearby (chop! chop!)
It shakes the ground
Under my pretty tree.

Look!
A strange little beast
With something in his paws
Coming into view—
I hope he likes bamboo.

Allow me to introduce myself
You probably don't know me
See, I don't get out that much
I just sit in my pretty tree
Sit in my pretty tree
Eating the tasty bamboo
Climb up and sit with me
Here in my pretty tree
There's room for us both you'll see
Here in my pretty tree.

I've Never Eaten
a Princess

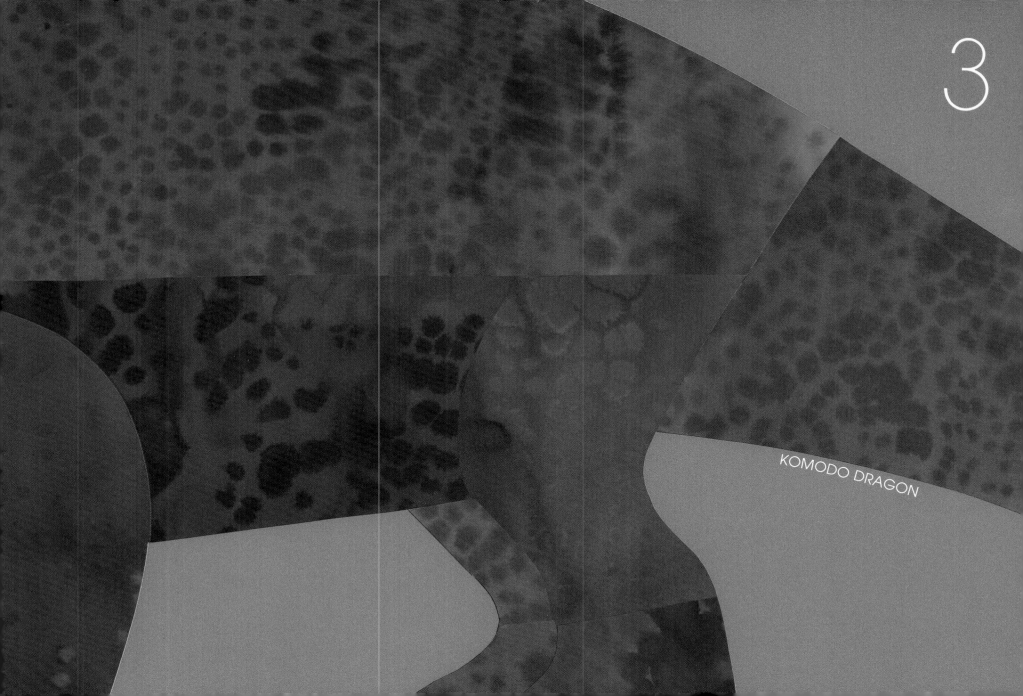

KOMODO DRAGON

I've never eaten a princess
Just the thought makes me sick
Surely her crown
Would get caught going down
And all of that taffeta — ick.

I've never eaten a princess
Not when there's plenty of goat
What with the frou-frou
And ticklish hairdo
Princess would stick in my throat.

There's a black cloud above me
Oh, what a terrible fate
No one will ever love me
All 'cause of someone I never ate.

I've never eaten a princess
I know that wouldn't be right
But fairy tales claim
That I am to blame
Whenever one drops
Out of sight.

I've never eaten a princess
Offer me one — I'll refuse
All skin and bones
Why I'd sooner eat stones
Than swallow those
Shiny red shoes.

There's a black cloud above me
Oh, what a horrible waste
No one will ever love me
All 'cause of someone
I wouldn't even taste.

I've never eaten a princess
Though you may think that's a lie
If ever I meet one —
A perfectly sweet one
The kind you would eat
If you wanted to eat one —
I'll look her right straight in the eye
And probably break down . . .
And cry.

I Am Not a Hat

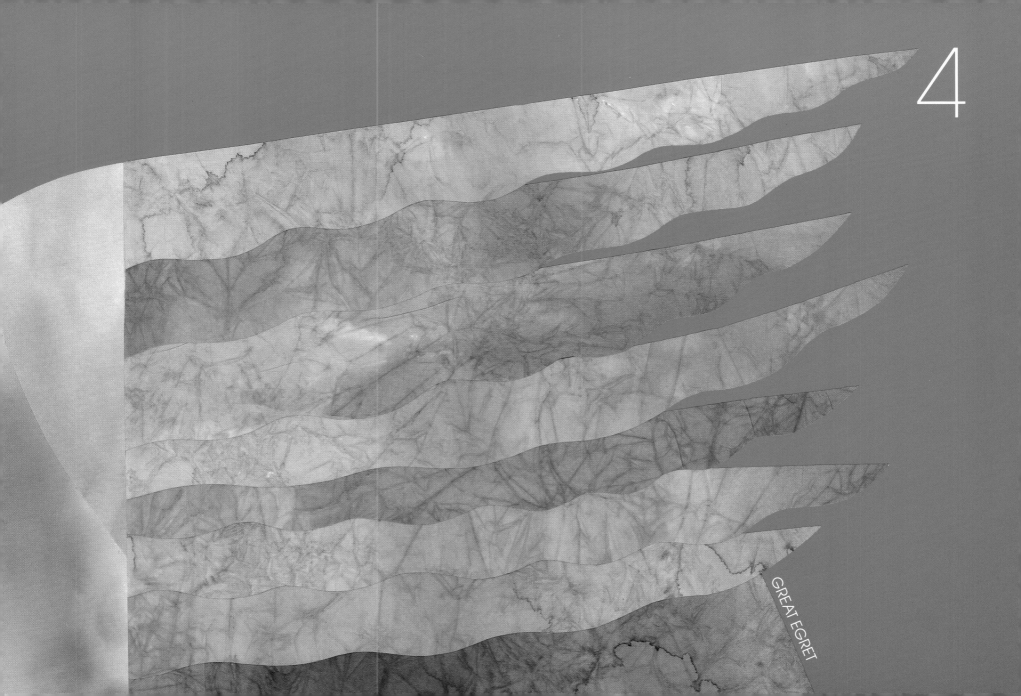

4

I am not a hat — no, I'm quite sure of that
I may be vain
I may be fat
But I am not a hat.

I'm perched upon a tree
Just the way a bird should be
But I can tell
That what you see
Is the hat you'd make of me.

Oh sure, it's true that with my feathers on
You'd make a lovely sight
But if it's you who's got my feathers on
What's to keep me warm at night?

I'll pull a worm for you to eat
I'll sing you songs unbelievably sweet
I'll catch you minnows with my feet
But then I really must repeat —

I know it's true that with my feathers on
You'd make a lovely sight
But if it's you who's got my feathers on
What's to keep me warm at night?

I am not a hat
I am a bird — you've got my word on that
And though your head looks nice and flat
It's not my natural habitat
No haberdashery would feel like home to me

For as you see
I am not a hat.

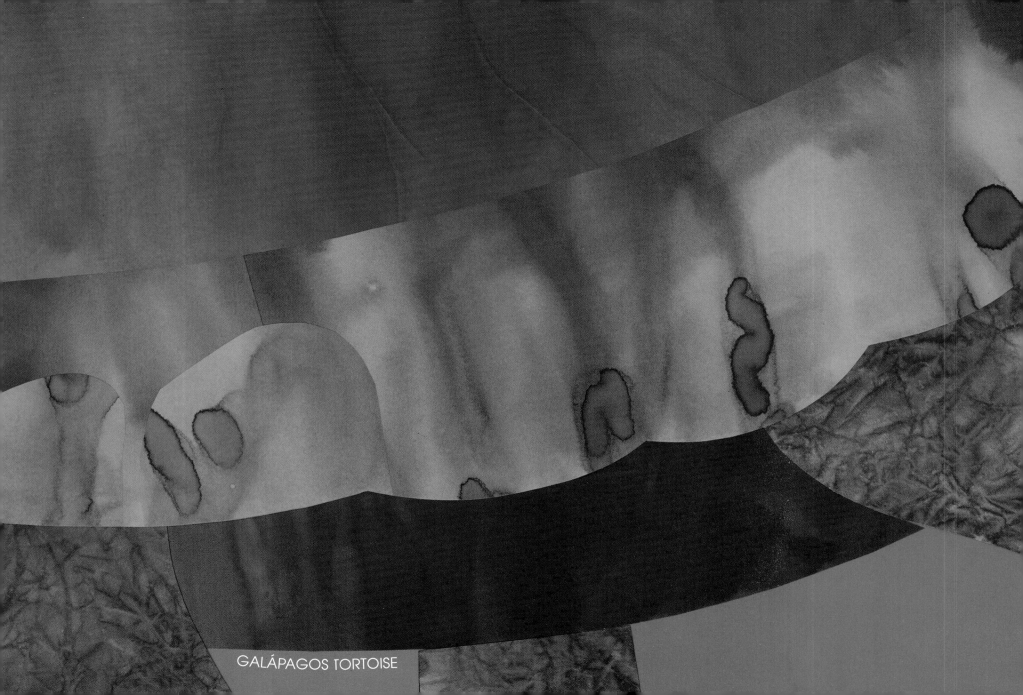
GALÁPAGOS TORTOISE

5

Take It Slow

Everybody's always running around saying
"Look at me! Look at me! Look at me!"
Everybody's always racing around saying
"Out of my way!"
I've been around awhile and there's one thing I know
Sometimes you've got to take it slow.

Everybody's always looking around saying
"Whatcha got? Whatcha got? Whatcha got?"
Everybody's always jumping around saying
"Give it to me!"
I've been around awhile and there's one thing I know
Sometimes you've got to take it slow.

Have you ever listened to a river's song?
Really, really listened the whole night long?
Nothing in your head but the rhythm of the flow
That's what it means to take it slow.

Everybody's always spinning around saying
"Give me more! Give me more! Give me more!"
Everybody's always scratching around saying
"Never enough."
I've been around awhile and there's one thing I know
Sometimes you've got to take it slow.

Take it from me . . .
I know.

Everybody's always turning around saying
"Where'd it go, where'd it go, where'd it go?"
Everybody's always shaking their heads saying
"What have we done?"
I've been around awhile and there's one thing I know
Sometimes you've got to take it slow.

Have you ever danced in fireflies' light?
Spinning like a fool on a summer's night
Nothing on your mind but the beauty of the glow
That's what it means to take it slow.

Take it from me . . .
I know.

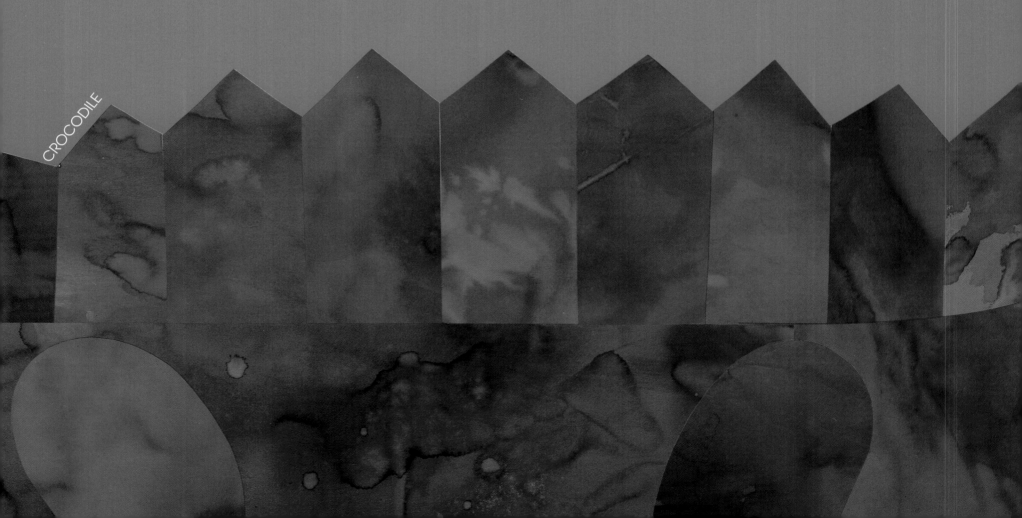

Crocodile Smile

CROCODILE

Don't be fooled by that crocodile smile.

What have I got to be happy about?
My sweetheart disappeared
And now I'm down and out
He left me high and dry in this swampy place
With nothing but the smile on my face
So I smile that crocodile smile.

All I do is sit here just grinning away
Even though I'm having one horrendous day
A perfect romance going up in smoke
And don't I look like I heard a good joke?
'Cause I smile that crocodile smile.

It must be nice to let your feelings show
It must be nice when other people know
It must be the best
To really be depressed
When everybody knows that you're blue
I'm just green with envy over you.

Even if I mustered up a salty tear
I'd still look really overjoyed from ear to ear
My honey up and left me and I've lost it all
But doesn't it look like I'm having a ball?
When I smile that crocodile smile.

When you're this unhappy
You get a little snappy
Every once in a while
So don't be fooled
By that crocodile smile.

TRICERATOPS SKELETON

Being Extinct

Being extinct isn't all it's cracked up to be
I'm just a dusty hunk of history
Nothing left of me but a bunch of bones
That some museum in Cleveland owns.

Being extinct is the loneliest game in town
Talking about it won't help — I'm really down
Just a flash in the pan — Now I am no more
Oh, why was I born a dinosaur?

Why didn't somebody help me
When the end was near
Why didn't somebody hold out a hand and say
"Here . . ."

Being extinct is a far cry from paradise
Back in the old days my life was nice
If I'd known I was headed for oblivion
Whoa, I would have grabbed my bones and run.

But there was no one to warn me
When the end was near
There was no one to hold out a hand and say
"Here . . ."

Being extinct isn't something I'd recommend
And it could happen again, my friend
It's not too late for the others — they won't disappear if you
Hold out your hand . . .
And say — "Here . . ."

TIGER

8

Pad, Pad, Pad

Pad, pad, pad . . .

Pad, pad through the tall green grass
Up the mountain and through the pass
Down to the river for a deep cool drink
And a little time to think.

Pad, pad through the noonday heat
Warm earth underneath my feet
Something wonderful fills the air
And I know I'm almost there.

Pad, pad, pad . . .

Pad, pad through the damp and lush
Crazy tangle of underbrush
To the place where the jungle ends
There I meet my friends.

Green eyes shining in the shadows
Green eyes narrow and so sly
Green eyes gaze at our new neighbors
Grazing in the meadow nearby.

Shake your stick little man, little man
Scare us off if you can
Maybe you can
But not for long.

Pad, pad, pad . . .

Pad, pad in the dark of night
Something moves in the pale moonlight
Nothing more than a nice cool breeze
Passing through those trees
Whispering . . . "Pad, pad, pad . . . "

I'm an Animal

I'm quiet as a mouse
I'm strong as an ox
Wise as an owl
Sly as a fox
Quick as a bunny
Crazy as a loon
And when I'm unhappy
I howl at the moon.

COMMON LOON

I'm vain as a peacock
Blind as a bat
They say I'm a birdbrain
They're right about that
Eager as a beaver
Stubborn as a mule
They say that I'm human
But I'm no fool.

WOOD DUCK

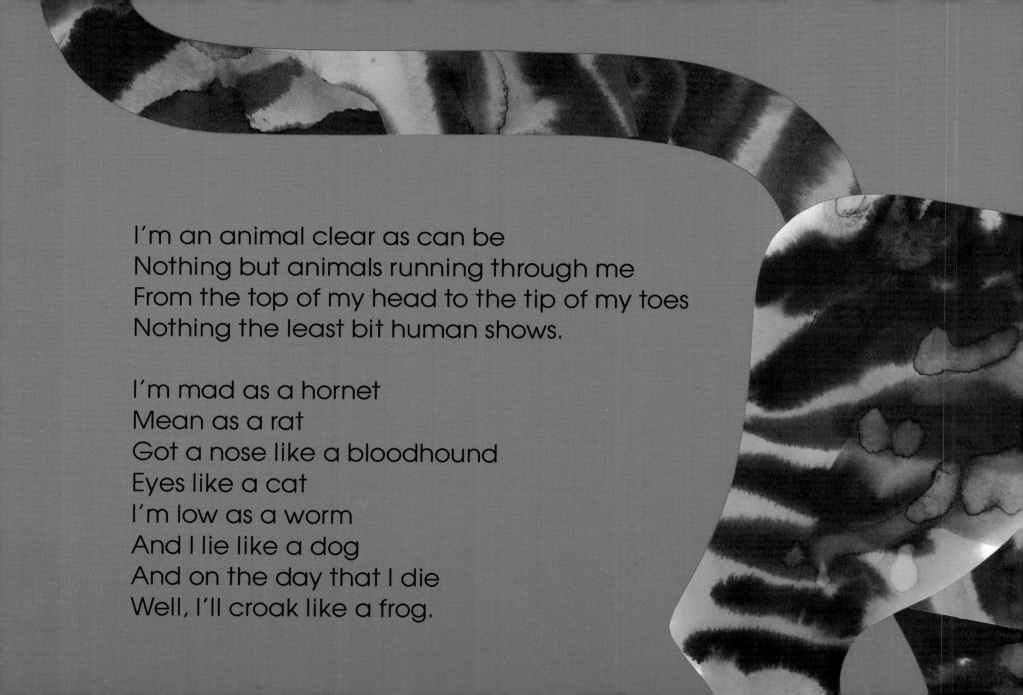

I'm an animal clear as can be
Nothing but animals running through me
From the top of my head to the tip of my toes
Nothing the least bit human shows.

I'm mad as a hornet
Mean as a rat
Got a nose like a bloodhound
Eyes like a cat
I'm low as a worm
And I lie like a dog
And on the day that I die
Well, I'll croak like a frog.

I'm an animal clear as can be
Nothing but animals running through me
From the top of my head to the tip of my toes
Nothing the least bit human shows.

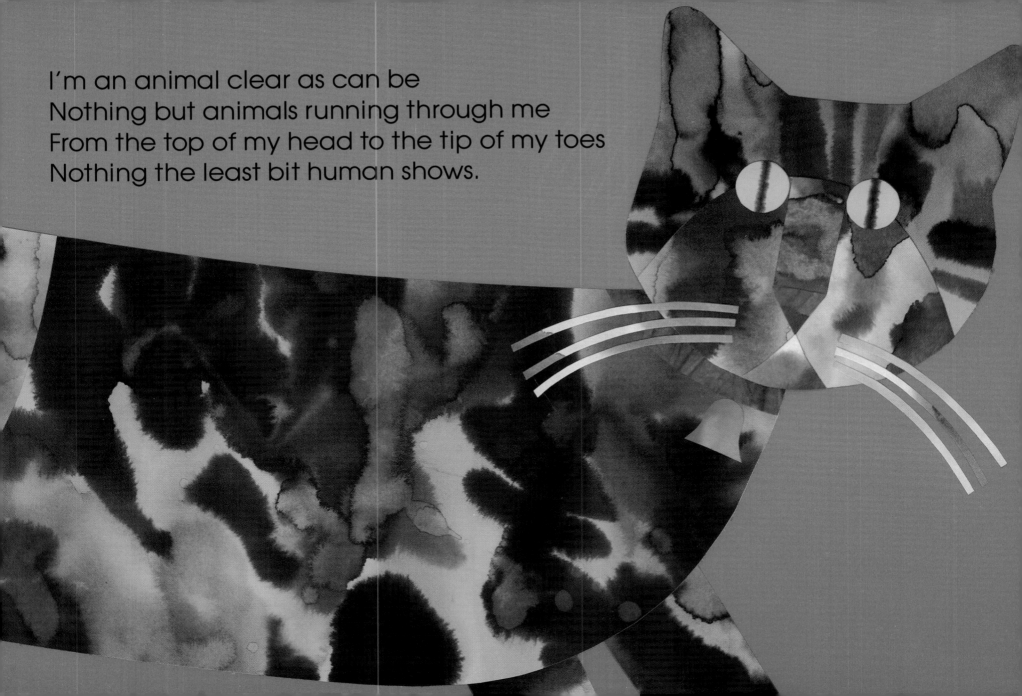

Let It Spin

Bumblebees need the blossoms to make their honey sweet
Blossoms need the bees to stir up the pollen with their feet
Isn't that a nice piece of work
Isn't it amazing the way the pieces fit
A nice piece of work, isn't it?

We breathe in and we breathe out many, many times a day
We breathe out — the trees breathe in
And they send it back our way
Isn't that a nice piece of work
Isn't it amazing the way the pieces fit
A nice piece of work, isn't it?

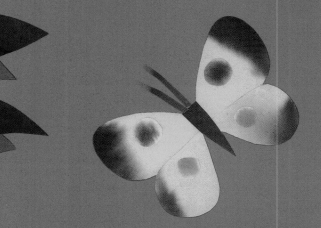

It's a perfect spinning circle
Balanced on a pin
Don't touch it, don't touch it
Let it spin.

All of us are children and nature is our mother
Each of us has a purpose so we all need one another
Isn't that a nice piece of work
Isn't it amazing the way the pieces fit
A nice piece of work, isn't it?

Baby, I need your loving to make it all worthwhile
The moon shines down on the love between us
And the two of us just smile
Isn't that a nice piece of work?
Isn't it amazing the way the pieces fit
A nice piece of work, isn't it?

It's a perfect spinning circle
Balanced on a pin
Don't touch it, don't touch it
Let's just let it spin.

10 Songs of the Earth as the Animals See It

1 Piece of Jungle
A tufted-eared marmoset tells about the animals, including humans, who call the jungle home.

2 Pretty Tree
A young giant panda listens to the "chop! chop!" of an axe as the man destroying his bamboo thicket gets closer and closer.

3 I've Never Eaten a Princess
A Komodo dragon bemoans the damage fairy tales have done to his reputation.

4 I Am Not a Hat
An egret does her best to discourage an admirer from using her feathers for a hat.

5 Take It Slow
A wise old Galápagos tortoise endorses life in the slow lane.

6 Crocodile Smile
A crocodile who's lost her mate laments her inability to show her true feelings.

7 Being Extinct
The skeleton of a triceratops shares a bit of firsthand experience.

8 Pad, Pad, Pad
A tiger following her instincts stalks the cattle grazing
in a field where jungle once stood.

9 I'm an Animal
What are humans made of?

10 Let It Spin
An anthem to the earth.

Crocodile Smile: 10 Songs of the Earth as the Animals See It   Text copyright © 1994 by Sarah Weeks.   Illustrations copyright © 1994 by Lois Ehlert.   Manufactured in China. All rights reserved.   www.harperchildrens.com   Library of Congress Cataloging-in-Publication Data Weeks, Sarah.   Crocodile smile: 10 Songs of the Earth as the animals see it / composed and performed by Sarah Weeks ; songbook illustrated by Lois Ehlert. p. cm. "Laura Geringer Books."   Contents: Piece of jungle—Pretty tree—I've never eaten a princess—I am not a hat—Take it slow—Being extinct—Pad, pad, pad—Crocodile smile—I'm an animal—Let it spin. ISBN 0-06-055745-1. — ISBN 0-06-056289-7 (lib. bdg.). 1. Children's songs—Texts.   [1. Animals—Songs and music.   2. Songs.] I. Ehlert, Lois, ill.   II. Title.   PZ8.3.W4125Cr 1994   782.42164'0268—dc20   94-3210 CIP AC New edition 2003